MW01193381

DIAL *M* FOR
Mother-in-Law

A Christmas in
July Novella

KIMBERLY KURTH GRAY

Year of the Book
135 Glen Avenue
Glen Rock, PA 17327

ISBN: 978-1-64649-350-0 (print)
ISBN: 978-1-64649-351-7 (ebook)

Chapter 1

It was the week before the fourth of July, Rehoboth Beach's busiest season. Mrs. North and I took advantage of a few more days of peace. Our end of the beach was never as crowded as it was nearer the hotels, but eventually people would spread out until there was scarcely any sand to see.

Mrs. North lay on a recliner, her face covered by a white veil, and her body tucked under a towel. "We mustn't let the sun age us, darling," she said to me every morning.

I sat on my blanket, sun lotion lathered on my already pink-tinged skin and reading over a few letters that had been sent into the paper for Mrs. North's advice column.

"Listen to this one," I said, then began to read from the note in my hand.

Dear Mrs. North,

My husband's family has not warmed up to me. We've been married for nearly three years and still they treat me as a guest, like I'm temporary. What can I do to get them to accept me as family? Please help.

Desperate in Dover

Mrs. North sighed. "Oh, darling. There's nothing she can do. I'd say it's her husband's fault. I suppose we can't write that, though." She pulled up her veil slightly to take a drag off her candy cane cigarette. "Let's write that family relationships take time to build, be patient. Advise her to be kind, helpful, and respectful, but not overly accommodating. She doesn't want to end up a doormat."

I took notes as Mrs. North went over each letter. There were thirty-six in all this time. The numbers seemed to be growing. Her column now ran twice a week instead of once, just to keep up with the demand. The paper allowed her to respond to three questions in each issue. At this rate, "Ask Mrs. North" was going to become a daily feature.

Nico paddled out on his board. Occasionally he'd give us a wave.

A few women walked down the beach calling, "Good morning," to us as they passed. It was hard to find a town friendlier than Rehoboth Beach.

After working a few hours, I helped Mrs. North carry our gear back to the house. She liked to have lunch served at noon. It was always the main meal of the day. I was preparing a Capri Salad and gazpacho, a cold soup I'd come to love. Before this job I hadn't been all that handy in the kitchen, but with Holly and Ivy—our house elves—on an extended leave to the North Pole, preparing the meals had become part of my daily jobs.

Nico came in just as I placed lunch on the table. "I was afraid I'd missed it," he said looking approvingly at the meal. "Let me get out of this." He pulled at his dripping wetsuit that left little to the imagination but a lot of water on the floor. Nico, with his buff body and man-bun, was nothing like the Santa I had read about in my childhood. "Want to help me?" he asked Mrs. North with a wink.

"Really, Nico," she said, her cheeks pinked, but she gave him a sly smile.

There are certain things you don't want to think about regarding Santa and Mrs. Claus, and *s-e-x* is definitely the major one. I busied myself arranging the napkins, pretending not to hear their banter.

A few minutes later we were all settled at the table enjoying our meals.

"Pass the pepper, Mother," said Nico.

"I am not your mother," Mrs. North answered sternly.

Nico just smiled. He enjoyed riling her up.

"I have our holiday planned," I announced as the couple dug into their salads.

While everyone else celebrated Independence Day, here at North Pole Beach we were having our first ever Christmas in July. As hard as Nico and Mrs. North worked to see that the world had a wonderful Christmas season, it wasn't much of a holiday for them. When they returned at daybreak on Christmas morning, a huge breakfast was served before the exhausted couple went to sleep, a sort of hibernation that lasted until Valentine's Day. I'd been frightened at first, holding a mirror to their noses just to be sure they were still breathing. I was relieved when they woke up as if they'd only slept for one night. Being the guardians of Christmas was hard work.

"On Friday evening we will have drinks on the patio before watching *It's a Wonderful Life* in the screening room," I began. "Saturday brunch will be followed by decorating the tree. I hope you don't mind, but our palm tree in the living room will have to make do. Then on Sunday after breakfast we'll see what Santa left in our stockings."

Mrs. North rolled her eyes.

"After dinner, presents will be exchanged. I'll serve drinks on the patio and we'll be just in time to watch the fireworks display. That will be a spectacular way to cap off our Christmas holiday."

"Good job, Natalie," Nico said. "And thanks for planning all of this."

"Yes, darling," agreed Mrs. North. "I'm actually excited about our little Christmas. I can't imagine why we haven't thought of it before now."

It made me happy to please them. I wasn't accustomed to getting things right. After leaving my job as a personal assistant to the Broadway actress—whom I refer to as Lady M—my self-esteem hit rock-bottom. Meeting Mrs. Doolittle and working at her temp agency had helped me to regain some faith in myself. Through her connections I landed this job with Mrs. North.

"You know, I was thinking we could..." Mrs. North said as the front doorbell chimed. And chimed. And chimed. "Who in the world could that be?" she asked and pushed her chair back from the table.

"Stay there, I'll see to it." I jogged down the hallway. The chime rang insistently. "Alright, already," I said and threw open the door.

4

Before me stood a woman dressed as a cowgirl. She wore a bright pink fringed vest, a pink and white cow-print skirt, and had a glittery pink scarf tied around her neck. Her bleached-blonde hair was piled high on her head in a beehive design. Mirrored aviator glasses hid her eyes.

"May I help you?" I asked. Who was I to judge her choice of outfit? If we could have a Christmas in July, she was certainly allowed to celebrate Halloween.

"Howdy, honey," she said. "Where's my baby?"

"I'm sorry, your baby?"

The woman pushed past me. "Nicholas, baby, Momma's here." She held her arms wide open and stood in the hallway like the statue of Christ the Redeemer on that peak in Brazil.

Nico appeared in seconds. "Momma?" Wide-eyed, he glanced at me then back at her before forming his face into a somewhat timid smile.

"Honey, I've missed you," she said and flung her arms around him.

Nico tried to extract himself from her embrace, but she was like an octopus with more arms than he could manage to untangle. "Missed you, too," he mumbled into her over-sprayed stiff hair.

"Give me some sugar," she said, lifting her cheek toward him which he dutifully pecked.

I noticed Mrs. North had yet to make an appearance. Moving past the mother and child reunion, I made my way back to the breakfast room where my lunch was waiting. Mrs. North sat at the end of the table, her arms crossed and her eyes like slits, glaring at Nico's vacant chair.

"Um, your mother... well, Nico's mother is..." I began to say but was interrupted.

"Just call me Jingle, honey," the woman said standing behind me. "And there she is, Queen Bee. How are you, Beira? Too tired to pull yourself out of that chair to greet an honored guest?"

Mrs. North sighed deeply. "I always welcome our guests, but then I realized it was only you."

"Jingle Belle Kringle," Nico's mom grabbed my hand and nearly shook it off my body. "Though some still refer to me as the real Mrs. Santa Claus. I'm a hard act to follow, honey."

"Jingle Belle. Dingle bell is more appropriate," Mrs. North said from behind the rim of her glass.

Nico cleared his throat, probably trying to absorb the sound of his wife's comment. "Momma, this is our assistant Natalie Tannon."

Jingle still clutched my hand, but stood back to give me a once over. "Very lovely," she said. "Isn't she lovely, Nico? And still young enough to have children. Do you like children, Natalie?"

"Not especially," I said and saw Mrs. North's mouth curl into a smile.

"Oh, pooh!" said Jingle. "Everyone loves children." She eyed Mrs. North. "Well, nearly everyone."

"Momma, why don't you take a seat?" Nico said, pulling out a chair. "We've only just started lunch. Natalie's made us a delicious salad and soup."

"Salad? Soup? What sort of meal is that? Where I come from, that's called the first course. Oh, honey," she said, turning to me. "You just sit yourself down.

Don't worry your pretty little head over meals. Jingle's here now and can cook us a proper feast."

Jingle made her way to the kitchen. We sat and stared at each other, listening as pots, pans, and utensils crashed and banged. The aroma of roasting beef filled the room, and within minutes Jingle reappeared.

"No wonder you're skin and bones. What's jolly about that?" She poked a finger in Nico's abs as she placed a tray of steaks on the table then carried out bowls of potatoes and baked beans. "Now we have ourselves a meal." Looking much pleased with herself, she sat at the end of the table and began plopping huge portions on Nico's plate.

"Momma, really, I shouldn't eat this way. I must be careful of my blood pressure."

"Honey, you don't look much like Santa, or even the boy I knew..." She stopped mid-sentence to throw Mrs. North a menacing snarl. "You look like some kind of yoga teacher. And that hair! What would the children think seeing you this way?"

"That's the point," Mrs. North said. "We want to be unrecognizable so that we may live our life in peace."

"You mean the life you want," Jingle said, spitting out the words along with a few beans. "You've never been interested in our family business. Your job is to support my son's work, not have a job of your own. What would my poor Claus think, God rest his soul. He worked his self to death for this job, for the children. If he could see his only son now, looking like some hippie and living in this hot climate."

"He wouldn't be able to see. He'd be passed out drunk," Mrs. North said, tossing down her fork.

"How dare you!" Jingle slammed her fist on the table.

"God rest his soul, alright. We should all be relieved that when he crashed the sleigh while driving intoxicated that he was the only fatality." Mrs. North stood. "It took nearly every elf in the fire brigade to recover his body from the wreckage."

Jingle began to sniffle. "Nicholas, are you going to let your excuse for a wife speak to me that way, and to besmirch the memory of your good father?"

Nico looked up from his plate. His spoon, nearly touching his lips, dripped with maple-glazed beans. "I, um, well... Dad did, you know, he did have an accident." Nico put the spoon down. "But, yeah, you know Bee, maybe we should change the subject."

Mrs. North tossed her napkin on her chair then walked through the breakfast nook. "Come along, Natalie. We have work to finish."

My stomach growled loudly, which brought a smile to Jingle's face. But my loyalty was to my employer, so I left the table and followed Mrs. North to her office. I thought about those delicious smelling beans for the rest of the day.

Chapter 2

"Should I buy some presents for Mrs.... um... Jingle?" I asked the next morning as Mrs. North and I settled ourselves in our usual beach spots.

We'd crept out of the house an hour earlier than normal. Jingle had already cornered Nico and was feeding him a "proper breakfast" of steak, eggs, fried tomatoes, and grits. He'd looked pleadingly at us as we snuck out the side door but didn't give away our departure. Not that Jingle was interested in spending time with Mrs. North.

She did, however, have a creepy fascination with me. She'd kept me up until well past my bedtime questioning me about my parents, my health, and my romantic entanglements. I had a sneaking suspicion she was sizing me up as a replacement for Mrs. North. Nope. Been there, done that. I wasn't about to ruin another perfectly fine job by marrying my boss's husband.

Nico had also been requested to stay up with us, but his end of the conversation amounted to nothing more than shaking or nodding his head, and an occasional, "Yes, Momma." The minute Jingle's eyes fluttered and she let out a yawn, Nico had bolted for the steps, but I hadn't been quick enough and was stuck another thirty minutes with her until she began to snore. I threw a light blanket across her lap and ran for my room like the devil was chasing me. In some ways I felt he had been.

"You were up rather late, darling," Mrs. North said, interrupting my reading of Frantic in Fenwick's letter. "Your eyes are all puffy. What in the world were you doing?"

What could I say? *Your mother-in-law was interviewing me for her son's second wife?* "I think Jingle needed company, someone to talk to."

Mrs. North sat up straighter, pulled up her veil, and slid her sunglasses down to the edge of her nose. "Is that so? What did she say?"

"Oh, nothing much."

"Natalie, I want to know every last word that came out of that... that bit... woman's mouth." Mrs. North patted the space next to her on the lounge chair and lit us each a candy cane cigarette.

We huddled together under the beach umbrella like schoolgirls at a sleepover.

"Really, it was all silly things," I said, choking a bit on the smoke.

"Like what?"

"You know, where I grew up and went to school, what my parents did for a living, had I been married, was I seeing anyone special now." I kept my eyes on the burning tip of the cigarette, not wanting to look at Mrs. North as I spoke. Surely, she would draw the same conclusions I had about Jingle's motives.

"She's a nosey old so and so." Mrs. North leaned back against the chair. "Everyone she meets she interrogates to see if they're... how does she put it? Her type of people. I'll tell you what." Mrs. North pointed an unlit candy cane at me. "She comes off as this grand lady of the manor, but I'm the one who came from a wealthy and influential family, not her. She's never even met her father." She cupped her hand around the cigarette to light it. I'd barely touched the one she'd given me. She really should cut down on her smoking.

"I'm sure she was just making conversation," I said.

"And another thing... she's always done her best to try to create a wedge between Nico and..." Mrs. North took the still unlit candy cane from her lips. "Wait a minute. Natalie, I think that wretched woman wants to replace me with you."

"See? I told you it was all silly. Let's not think about her. It's a beautiful day, we're out of the house, and there's an entire bag of letters to answer."

I smiled, but the words were still hanging in the air when clouds covered the sun. Then I realized it was only Jingle's shadow.

"Thought I'd join the girls," said Jingle. "Put it right there, honey," she said to Nico who carried a chair strapped to his back, with an umbrella under one arm and a picnic basket slung over the other.

After setting up the chair and umbrella, Nico took off like a shot, diving into the ocean, no surfboard needed.

"He's nothing but skin and bones," Jingle said, shedding her wrap to reveal a leopard print bikini.

I wanted to look away but couldn't. It was both fascinating and disturbing. She perched on her lounge chair, snow-white skin reflecting the sun into my eyes. Once again she wore her aviator shades and my shocked expression was mirrored in them.

"You're going to need sunscreen," I told her. "Lots and lots of sunscreen." I pulled the tube from my bag and handed it to her.

"Now aren't you a thoughtful person," said Jingle. "Isn't she thoughtful, Beira?"

"So thoughtful," Mrs. North said. "You'll see though that Natalie and I have work to do."

"Don't mind me. I'm zipping it and locking it," said Jingle, doing the motions of zipping and locking her lips and throwing away the key. "You won't hear a peep out of me."

"Good," said Mrs. North.

"Not a word."

"We are working," Mrs. North reminded her.

"Silent as a mouse on Christmas Eve."

"Now, Natalie, that last letter." Mrs. North motioned to the mail bag that sat on the sand at our feet.

"If it's one thing I'm known for, it's being quiet," continued Jingle. "I can keep a secret, too. When Freda in Dolls and Accessories told me she was having feelings for her supervisor—you know that little guy Herbie? Well, I was surprised, but I didn't say a word, not one word. I kept quiet, kept my mouth tightly shut. And when his wife asked if I'd seen him, did I blurt out that he was being unwrapped by Freda in the gift department? I did not. I stayed silent. So, you can see—or rather *hear,* I suppose—that I know when it's time to talk and when it's time to keep my lips still."

Mrs. North and I stared at her then at each other, both of us with our mouths slightly open.

Jingle began humming to herself, seemingly unaware of our reaction to her words.

"Alright then, about this woman in Fenwick," Mrs. North said, but never had a chance to finish her thought.

"I knew a man once; his last name was Fenwick. John Fenwick. Or was it James?" Jingle giggled. "Either way, he was handsome, I mean mighty handsome," said Jingle and leaned toward me, placing her hand on my arm. "Not as handsome as my Nicholas, mind you. I bet you've never seen anyone as handsome as my son, have you, Natalie?"

My face became red, and it wasn't from the sun. I knew from experience that Mrs. North could read my mind, as she had on many occasions. With Jingle's words, an image of Nico formed—in his muscle-hugging wetsuit emerging from the ocean, droplets of water clinging to his long hair. I could feel my heart pounding. I wanted to stop, but I couldn't. It was as if I had no control over it.

"Come along, Natalie," Mrs. North's steely voice snapped me out of my daydream.

I picked up our bags and scurried across the beach after her like a sand crab without a shell.

She was already in her office and behind her desk by the time I came panting into the house.

"Close the door, will you?" she asked, then pointed at the chair next to her.

"I swear to you, I have absolutely, positively no designs on your husband. I mean, I like Nico just fine, and..."

"Natalie, stop." Mrs. North pulled a bottle of peppermint schnapps from the bottom drawer of her desk. She poured a shot for me and one for her. "Bottoms up," she said and clinked her glass to mine.

"It's not five o'clock anywhere," I said after the burning in my throat cooled. What was happening to me? It wasn't even lunchtime yet and I was smoking and drinking like a college student.

"Natalie, darling, you've done nothing wrong. It's her. She's an evil, meddlesome..." Mrs. North let out a growl. "The thoughts you were having about Nico. She put them in your head. That's what she does, gets into your mind and soon enough you start believing that maybe, just maybe the boy down the street whom you've despised all your life is the man of your dreams."

"Jingle has the power to control my thoughts?" I was horrified. Maybe I didn't want to eat beans after all.

"Not always. Her main focus is romance. She snipes at me for having a job when I know very well what she does in her free time."

"What?" I wanted to know and scooched my chair closer to the desk. "What does she do in her free time?"

"Just what I told you. She convinces people who loathe each other that they're soulmates. Then she

14

writes it all down and sends it to her friend who's a producer at that television station that shows Christmas movies all year long. You know the ones— girl loses big city job, moves back home to the farm, reconnects with boy who made her childhood unbearable, swears she can't stand the farm, him, or her mother, but amongst all the sparkling Christmas lights realizes he's her soulmate and there's no place like home on the farm."

"Jingle writes those movies?" I asked.

"Every sugary, sickening sweet moment of them." Mrs. North made a face like her teeth were in pain.

"Does she get paid for this work?" I asked.

"Of course. She needs the money for her high living lifestyle. She likes to have the best of everything. What people think of her is more important than almost anything." Mrs. North's mood became more somber. "If she didn't cause so many problems and work as hard as she does to undermine my marriage, I might feel differently about her. I know her life hasn't been easy."

"Even if that's true, that's no excuse for how she treats you, or how she's trying to manipulate me," I said. "I mean, how hard could her life possibly be?"

Mrs. North sat staring at her hands for a few seconds. "She grew up without a father. Worse yet, he was world-renowned for spreading love."

"Who's her father?" I asked.

Mrs. North leaned over her desk and whispered, "Cupid."

Seriously? *Cupid?* It was true that I'd had to accept many fantastical situations over the past nine months since accepting this position with Mrs. North. I mean, who would believe me if I told them I work for Mr. and Mrs. Santa Claus? They'd either presume I worked at some sort of holiday-themed store or that I was off my nut. I've learned to not only live with this secret, but to relish it. It makes me feel rather special, or like I'm some sort of secret agent. But now Mrs. North was going to throw Cupid in the mix? What would be next? Will the Tooth Fairy turn out to be her niece?

"Cupid? The little cherub with a bow and arrow depicted on greeting cards everywhere in February. You're telling me that little angel is Nico's grandfather?"

"He's no angel, darling. More of a demon," said Mrs. North. "The public has simply no idea what they've gotten themselves into by promoting him and his nasty games. Trust me, the last thing any of us needs is to be struck by his venomous arrow."

"But, but..." I stuttered. "I thought he promoted peace and love. He's the poster boy for romance."

"His version of romance," Mrs. North said with a sigh. "Darling, he has outdated ideas—ones that should have stayed with Raphael in the Renaissance."

"But he's so cute, and tiny. How much trouble could he cause?"

"You'd be surprised to learn how many children he's fathered. No thought to their upbringing. He just goes along doing as he pleases. He seems to take pleasure in disrupting peoples' lives. Shoots arrows and brings together couples who should never have shared a cup of coffee let alone a mortgage and children. So many have suffered because of his whims."

Had this been the reason I'd fallen in love with Lady M's husband Felix? It was true that I hadn't paid him much thought until one afternoon the elevator doors slid open in her penthouse and there he stood, just as he'd done every single afternoon for two years. Only that time the sunlight surrounded him, casting blue and green light over him from Lady M's bottle collection. He looked like a piece of stained glass come to life. Even today I remember how my heart began to pound, and I felt as if I might faint.

"Natalie, are you alright?" Mrs. North was kneeling next to me, holding my hand. She sat back on her heels. "We need to send Jingle on her way. I can tell her visit is already disturbing you."

Chapter 3

*I*t seemed Jingle meant to stay, at least long enough to celebrate our Christmas in July. Mrs. North suggested an outing would do me good and help clear my head of all Jingle had clogged in it.

I strolled down the boardwalk taking in the fresh, salty air. It was still early enough in the day to be quiet. Most families were enjoying breakfast at Robin Hood's or cycling around on bicycles made for two.

I made my way down to Browseabout Books. A good cup of coffee and a chat with my friend Jessie was just what was needed. Several people stood in line, but I was in no hurry. Mrs. North had insisted I take the morning off.

I waved to Jessie who was helping a customer and took my place at the back of the line.

My turn was next when I decided a cookie would be perfect with my coffee. I stepped to the side to decide what to select.

"I'll have..." I heard a man say.

"Excuse me. It's my turn," I said, holding a prepackaged snickerdoodle.

"You weren't in line," he said to me.

"I most certainly was in line. I was choosing a sweet."

"Look, you weren't in line and I'm in a hurry. I have to get to work."

"Go ahead then," I said, but couldn't help my huffy tone.

"I need four black coffees, two lattes with oat milk, one mocha latte with coconut milk, and an iced caramel latte, no whip."

"You've got to be kidding me," I said.

The man didn't respond. He didn't even thank me for letting him cut in line, not that I'd done so willingly.

Finally, he moved to the end of the counter so I could place my order. I watched him from the corner of my eye. He was rather tall with dark wavy hair. Why was it that every handsome man I met had an attitude problem? I ordered my usual vanilla latte with oat milk and a drizzle of caramel and stalked over to where Jessie stood near her desk.

"Men," I said, and nodded toward the door where Mr. Rude pushed his way outside, balancing his coffee order.

"Him? Yeah, he comes here often. He's mostly a window shopper, frowns a lot." Jessie laughed. "You're here bright and early today. Slow at work?"

"Something like that," I smiled. I'd become good friends with Jessie, but even she didn't know the secrets of my job. "Think I'll take a look around. Has the new Elly Griffiths come in yet?"

"Next week," Jessie said before being called on by an associate. "Talk to you later." Then she disappeared amongst the aisles of books.

After a sip of latte and a friendly face, I was feeling better already.

The walk and bookstore had done wonders for me, but no matter how hard I tried, I couldn't avoid Jingle. She insisted on "helping" me with all the preparations for our upcoming Christmas in July, which actually meant she did everything her way, and my agenda was totally scrapped.

"We don't want to watch *It's a Wonderful Life*. It's overrated and depressing, don't you think? Now what we need is a good comedy. How about *Elf*? Oh, I know, honey. Let's watch *The Christmas Chronicles*. That Kurt Russell sure is a cutie!"

"I thought a more traditional..." but I never managed to complete a full sentence when she was around.

"Boring," she sang out. "Christmas should be fun, exciting, entertaining. I know these guys; they dress up like elves. They're not really elves, too tall, but they dance, bring their own boom box and chairs, and poles, everything they need. My, and are they ever handsome." Jingle smacked her lips together and made a sound I never want to hear again. "Of course, not as handsome as my boy, but you know that."

Mrs. North had explained to me that whenever I was near Jingle and she began to talk about Nico, I was to visualize the saddest thing I could. Now, my mind was on the rabbit I'd run over ten minutes after passing my driver's exam. I hope Mrs. North won't someday reveal he was the Easter Bunny.

"Are these men strippers?" I asked.

A sly grin crossed Jingle's face. "Exotic dancers. Beira will love it."

Before I could come up with a snappy reply, or even pick my jaw up from the floor, the front doorbell chimed. I sat the box of crystal icicles on the table and headed down the hallway, a sense of déjà vu hovering in the air. Ever since the arrival of Jingle, the sound of a doorbell caused my anxiety to peek.

The silhouette of a man shadowed the shaded window. I opened the door but left the chain in place. No one was getting past me again. "Can I help you?"

"Hello, there," the man said, tilting his head as if playing peek-a-boo with a child. "I'm here to see Mrs. Kringle, er, Jingle."

Was he one of the exotic dancers she'd told me about? He was rather handsome with his wind-blown gray hair and icy-blue eyes. Could I say he had the wrong house and send him on his way? Any friend of Jingle's had to be bad news. "She's..."

"Jack? Jack, honey is that really you? Oh, you naughty boy! You must stop following me." Jingle pulled me away from the door and swung it open, ripping the chain from the wall. "Get in here and give me some sugar."

For his part, the man called Jack looked as bewildered as I felt. Jingle threw her arms around his neck and planted a kiss on his cheek so hard the smack might have been heard all the way in Ocean City.

Jack rubbed his face which now appeared to have Jingle's lips tattooed on it. "Yes, well, I was passing by, on my way to Atlantic City," he said pointedly to me. "Thought I might pop in and see my old friend Jingle Belle."

Jingle's smile drooped a bit at the word "old" but regained its sparkle when she noticed me watching her. "Come in, come in," she said and steered him into the living room. "Natalie, bring us a couple of iced teas, won't you, honey?"

"Extra ice for me, please," Jack said.

I slammed two tall glasses on the counter and filled them with ice that sweat in my hot hands. Was I now working for Jingle as well? I sliced lemons, added more ice to make up for the melted pieces, then poured the tea. With everything on a tray, I went back to the living room.

"I told you. All our business was to be over the phone. What if you're seen?" I heard Jingle say.

I paused behind the large palm tree. Jingle's voice was razor-sharp, not at all her usual sugar-sweet tone. This Jack was definitely not an exotic dancer.

"I'm not staying. You know I hate all of this sun and hot weather, but I had to get a feel for the place, see how everything is laid out," Jack told her.

I took a few quiet steps backward and called out, "Shall I bring cookies as well?"

"None for me," Jack answered.

I brought the tray in, and Jingle shook her head. "No, no, no. I like mint, not lemon. Is this sweet tea? I only drink sweet tea."

Jack shrugged and rolled his eyes. "I'll drink what you've so kindly brought."

After Jingle refused hers, Jack took both glasses. I marched back into the kitchen to brew fresh tea and add sugar. What was it with these women from the North Pole and their love of mint?

I returned to the living room with the new tea to find Jack alone, studying a photograph of Mrs. North and Nico. It was from their wedding and had yellowed with age. People paid for similar photos on the boardwalk where they dressed you in costumes and posed you as sheriffs and saloon girls.

His smile widened as he turned toward me. "Thank you," he said, taking yet another glass from me. "It's Natalie, right?" Our fingers touched and a chill ran through my body. It was nice, like a dip in cool water on a hot day.

"Where's Jingle?"

"She's run off on some crazy errand, but you were going to such trouble to please her, so I thought it a shame to have your efforts wasted."

I didn't want to smile or show I was pleased in any way, but my face muscles were not cooperating, and I couldn't seem to remove my silly grin. "Thank you," I said, unable to stop staring into those blue eyes of his. "It really wasn't that much trouble." Now I sounded like some giggly teenaged girl. What was wrong with me?

"Why don't we sit down?" Jack took the chair next to the bookshelf. "You know, the name Natalie doesn't really suit you. I feel something lighter would be more fitting. I'm going to call you Talia. Would you mind?" he asked as I plopped on the edge of the couch.

"Talia? That's sort of like a nickname and rather lovely. No, I wouldn't mind at all." I could feel the heat racing up my neck and across my face.

It was a strange feeling, sitting here in the living room like a guest. I spent most of my time in Mrs. North's office or the kitchen, stumbling up to my bed for several hours of sleep before starting all over again. "I only have a minute," I said, smoothing down the hem of my dress.

Suddenly I was conscientious of my appearance, something I hadn't given much thought to in years. I wore my hair in a bun now since cooking had become one of my jobs. No one likes a dish seasoned with curls. Make-up also became irrelevant. I only own lip gloss these days.

"Talia" seemed too fancy a name for me, but it did give me a bit of a thrill. There was something romantic and exciting about this man Jack.

"Have you worked here long for Bee..., I mean Mrs. North?

It's been roughly nine months," I said, and couldn't help but to check my watch. "Look, I really need to get some things accomplished before Mrs. North returns."

"Could I help you with anything?" Jack glanced at the discarded box of crystal icicles. "I'm actually quite good at hanging icicles."

"Don't you have someplace to be?" I asked.

"All of that can wait," he said, picking up the box. "These are for the tree, I suspect," Jack nodded at the half-decorated palm that stood near the doorway.

"Yes, we're doing up the house for a Christmas in July party... just for fun." How much did Jack know about Jingle? I had to be careful about what I said.

Jack didn't seem to think it odd we were decorating the house for Christmas in the midst of a heat wave. He took the box and gingerly hung the icicles on the tree. "If you'd be so kind as to fetch me another cold drink, I'd certainly appreciate it," he said.

"Of course. Extra ice?" I couldn't stop smiling.

"You know me so well already."

I hurried off to the kitchen to fetch a large glass of ice water. It was hot even though the air conditioner seemed to be running overtime. The air was actually chilly in the living room. By the time I returned, Jack had the tree entirely decorated with icicles, sparkling beads that appeared to be snowdrops and lace snowflakes. Where had they come from? The tree was stunning.

"Wow," was the only thing I could say. "I had no idea a palm tree could be this Christmassy. Where did you find the snowflake ornaments?" I traced my finger around one. It was cold and fragile, and for a second, I worried it would melt.

"I wouldn't touch them. They're antiques, I'm sure. I found them under the tissue, beneath the icicles."

"All we need now is a few lights," I said.

Jack shook his head. "No lights. These ornaments will glow all on their own. Why don't I come back this evening and take you to dinner? The tree will be in its glory after sunset, you'll see."

"Oh well, thanks so much for helping me, and for the dinner invitation, but I really can't go. One of my responsibilities is to make dinner for Mrs. North and I need to be here to get things together."

"Late dinner then?" He put his hand on mine and gave it a tiny squeeze. "I'll be back at eight. See you then, Talia."

I opened my mouth to decline again, but only the word "Okay" croaked out. Was this a date? Had I just agreed to a date? How would I ever explain this to Mrs. North?

Chapter 4

Mrs. North was in her office after her motorcycle ride with Nico to Ocean City. Once a week they drove down Route One to Belly Busters for lunch. Mrs. North would return home, her usually sleek bob a mass of sweaty curls from the helmet.

As she sat at her desk combing out her hair I gave her the phone messages and mail. "By the way, would you mind if I went out this evening for a few hours?" I asked as casually as my dry throat would allow,

"Darling, your evenings are your own," she said, but we both knew this wasn't really true. "Hot date?" she asked, giving me a sideways glance.

"I'm not sure. I met this man today, a friend of Jingle's. He invited me to a late dinner. Jack said..."

"Jack?" Mrs. North dropped her comb. "A friend of Jingle's? What does this Jack look like?"

"He's a bit taller than me, thin, silvery-gray hair, light blue eyes, a trim beard."

"No. You may not go with him. You're not allowed." Mrs. North slammed her hand on the desk. "We have important work to do tonight."

"I wouldn't go out until my work was finished. You know that." I was worried she was thinking of sending me to my room and grounding me for the rest of the week. "I never let my personal life interfere with my job."

Mrs. North arched her eyebrow.

"Okay, let me amend that statement. I've never let my personal life interfere with my work since I've been here." I sat in the chair opposite her desk. "I haven't been out in ages, let alone on a date. This is the first time I've asked for a night off."

Mrs. North watched me for a second. "I know that's true, Natalie, and it's not that I don't want you to have friends and enjoy yourself. I'm saying this for your own good."

"You're beginning to sound a lot like my mother."

"This man, Jack, he isn't who, or what you think. He's not even... that doesn't matter. I know Jack, and I have for many more years than I care to recall. Nothing good comes from his arrival. He may seem handsome and smart, and you may believe now that you want to be with him, but darling his luster soon wanes. Under that sleek exterior is nothing but slush."

"It's only dinner. I'm not going to marry him. Besides, he's only passing through on his way to Atlantic City."

"You're a grown woman and I can't tell you what to do or whom to see, but as your employer... as your friend... I would like you to take my words seriously. Jack is not a... well, he's not to be trusted."

There was no need for me to worry about preparing dinner. Jingle stood at the stove in a pair of wedged sandals, a purple halter dress with rhinestone buttons, and her hair piled on her head like that leaning tower in Pisa. "Sit on down, honey. I'll get you a plate. I've made grits, collard greens, chicken-fried steak, and mashed sweet potatoes."

Nico and Mrs. North sat side by side at the table, not in their usual spots, like naughty children awaiting punishment.

"No thanks, no dinner for me this evening. I'm going out." I glanced at Mrs. North, but she kept her eyes on her plate.

"Honey, you got a beau," said Jingle. "Well, good on you. Though I had someone particular in mind for you."

Rather than give in to her provocation, I let visions of dead rabbits fill my head. "Not a date," I said pointedly to Mrs. North. "Not a beau, just a casual dinner with a new friend."

"That's a relief. I'd hate to see you with the wrong person when the right man is so close at hand." Jingle took Nico's empty plate and exchanged it for one overflowing with food. "Don't stay away too long. I thought we'd have a cozy drink on the veranda tonight. You wouldn't want to miss that, now, would you?"

"I'm sure Ja—"

"Have a good time," Mrs. North said loudly, drowning out the rest of my words.

Jingle stopped dishing out food and turned to me, an odd expression on her face, something between shock and anger. The plate in Jingle's hand dropped, hitting the floor with a crash, sending shards of pottery over the tiles.

"Momma, are you okay?" Nico asked.

"Fine, slippery plate is all." Jingle bent to pick up the glass, but Nico shooed her away and brushed everything up.

"Go on, Natalie. You don't want to be late." Mrs. North pointed at the door.

I went hurriedly out of the house and down the walkway, meeting Jack as he pulled up. It seemed Jack was something both Jingle and Mrs. North agreed on—neither wanted Nico to know he was in town.

I slid into the front seat of Jack's silver Jaguar. The drive to the restaurant was too short. I loved the feel of the leather seats and enjoyed the smooth ride, though the air conditioner was on so high I was half frozen. It was a pleasure to step out into the humidity again to warm up.

"I hope you like French food," Jack said, placing his hand at the small of my back and guiding me to the entrance.

La Fable was a restaurant I'd wanted to try, but never managed to get there. The waiter appeared before we even had our napkins unfolded and Jack ordered a bottle of champagne with Steak Tartare and Oeufs Mimosa for hors d'oeuvres.

"I hope you don't mind that I've ordered for us," he said, gazing at me through the candlelight, then blowing it out.

"Not at all," I said, but I was uneasy. This all seemed a bit overly romantic for a first date, if it was indeed a date. *Think dead rabbits*, I said to myself, *and take it slow.* "I pass by here often enough, but I've never been in. My usual spot is Jam, but it's been a long time since I've been there."

"You need to take care of yourself, Talia. Don't let Bee, I mean, Mrs. North, or Jingle for that matter, overwork you."

"I don't work for Jingle. I'm employed by Mrs. North, though occasionally I help Nico."

"Ah, Nico," he said with what appeared to be a grimace.

"You don't like him?" I asked. Who wouldn't like Nico? Right there I decided I could never be interested in anyone who didn't like Santa Claus, er... Nico. Just like that, the vision hit me again. Nico emerging from the ocean, his wetsuit missing. Oh no! "Dead rabbit! Dead rabbit!"

"You want rabbit?" asked Jack, his face pinched with confusion.

"No, I saw something..." I covered my words with a slight laugh and waved my hand in front of me. "It was nothing. Sorry. I'll have whatever you think is best." Whatever he thought best? Who am I? What was happening to me?

When the waiter returned with our hors d'oeuvres and popped the cork on the champagne, Jack ordered Poulet Cordon Bleu for me and Beef Bourguignon for himself. "We can both have a little of each entrée," he said.

The food was delicious. I ate even after I was full. I didn't want to leave a crumb. Jack asked me about my work and was attentive, especially when I told him about my years working as a personal assistant for the famous Broadway actress Lady M. I left out the parts about being married to her husband twice, but if he read any newspapers, he already knew about that.

It wasn't until we were walking to the car that I realized he'd not said a single word about his life or line of work. "I'm sorry, I seem to be hogging the conversation. Tell me about yourself. Where do you live? What do you do for a living? How do you know Jingle?"

Jack held his hands in front of him as if to ward off my questions. "Slow down," he said and chuckled a bit. I liked the sound of his laugh. "I guess you could say I'm a meteorologist."

"Like a weatherman? Are you on television?"

"No, I work behind the scenes."

"Oh, you're a scientist."

"Something like that, yes. I work mostly with cold weather, snow, sleet, that sort of thing. I travel, haven't ever really settled down... not yet at least." He gave me a look of longing as he spoke those words. "And I know Jingle, and your Mrs. North, and Nico, as you call him, from my hometown."

"You're from the North Pole? You're a bit tall for an elf," I said.

"I'm not an elf. I'm whatever I want to be. Right now, I want to be a man here with a beautiful woman."

I couldn't help myself. I blushed. How long had it been since any man had noticed me, let alone called me beautiful? "You're too kind, and apparently need glasses."

"My eyes work perfectly well, thank you." As we approached the car, Jack stopped and turned to face me. "I like you, Talia, and I hope you like me. I really have no pressing commitments at the moment, and I'd like to stick around a few more days, if you would be interested in going out with me again."

"That would be nice," I said. I got into the car and Jack went around to the driver's side.

We drove the short distance back to North Pole Beach in silence. Once outside the house, Jack placed his hand on mine. "Will you be free tomorrow night?"

"I can be."

"Good. Then how about I meet you at Jam? Will seven o'clock work?"

"Let's say eight. We can meet at the bar for drinks."

"Eight o'clock it is then." He leaned across the seat and kissed me lightly on the lips. "And Talia?"

"Mmm?" I murmured. I was having a vision of being held in his arms as sparkling snowflakes danced around us.

"Would you mind terribly keeping our meetings between the two of us?"

I opened my eyes and stared at him. "Are you married? Tell me now. I don't date married men." *Anymore*, I thought, but didn't say that part.

He laughed. "No, I'm not married now, nor have I ever been. I, well, the truth is I'd rather Jingle not know I was still in town. She can be a bit..."

"Overbearing? Bossy? In your business?"

"Yes, all the above. I don't want her to interfere with whatever might develop between us. Is that alright with you?"

"Absolutely." This time I leaned across the seat and kissed him until the stars turned into snowflakes and my lips felt frozen to his.

Chapter 5

Mrs. North was standing at the bottom of the steps when I came in the door. She put her finger to her lips and waved me down the hall into her office. Inside she shut the door and turned on the sound machine and the radio to a jazz station.

"She hates jazz," Mrs. North said and lit up one of her candy cane cigarettes. She offered the pack to me, but I begged off. "How was your date? How is Jack?"

I did my best to conjure up the thought of dead rabbits, hoping it would keep Mrs. North from reading my mind, but she didn't seem to notice or care. "He's fine. We went to La Fable for dinner. Everything was excellent."

"You like him, don't you?"

"We had a nice time. He's quiet, but polite and seemed interested in all I said."

"Darling, be careful there. He's not what you think. He can be extremely charming one minute, and ice cold the next. Believe me, I've experienced both."

"Yes, he told me the North Pole is his hometown and that's how he knows Jingle, you, and Nico."

"What else did he say, about me, I mean?"

I watched Mrs. North as she studied the tip of her cigarette, pretending not to be interested, but I could sense she was the opposite.

"That was it. He said he was from the North Pole, that's all."

"Nothing about our school years, or any of that?"

"School years?" How old was this guy? "No, not a word."

Mrs. North leaned over conspiratorially toward me and lowered her voice to a mere whisper. "We were sweethearts, had promise rings, courted, and nearly married."

I sank into the chair near her desk. Would this forever be my fate? All the men in this world and I was seemingly destined to always entwine myself with my bosses' husbands or boyfriends. "He didn't tell me any of that."

"Jingle hasn't said a word about him. She wouldn't say anything in front of Nico. He and Jack had a violent confrontation the day of our wedding. Jingle, though she takes great pleasure in irritating me, would not upset her Nicholas for the world."

"If you don't mind me asking, why did Jack and Nico argue? Was it over you?"

"Why of course it was, darling," said Mrs. North looking more pleased than distressed over the memory. "Jack thought he still had a chance to win me back. Jingle had naturally set it all in motion. She never liked me or wanted me to marry Nico. Do you think...?"

"Think what?" I asked.

"Not to sound too full of myself, but do you think I'm the reason Jack's here? Could Jingle have convinced him to fall in love with me again? Oh, that dreadful woman."

"I promise he said nothing about you, nothing at all. Anyway, he told me he's going to Atlantic City, so there's no need for you to worry."

"I'm not worried, darling, merely curious as to what my dearest mother-in-law is cooking up. I guarantee you it's more than our meals."

After tossing and turning for over an hour, I convinced myself I was hungry. I couldn't possibly be after the dinner I ate, but there I was riffling through the freezer searching for the pint of coffee fudge ice cream I'd hidden. I needed ice cream. I deserved it. How could I allow myself, once again, to be attracted to a man whose heart belonged to another? Would I never learn?

I had a real problem, one that needed more counseling and advice than Mrs. North's column could supply. I pulled a spoon from the drawer and was scooping out a hunk when the stairwell light went on and someone creeped down the steps. Not wanting to get a lecture from Mrs. North about eating in the middle of the night or how my liver needed twelve hours rest each day, I tucked myself away in the broom closet.

Peering through the crack in the door, I saw it wasn't Mrs. North but Jingle. She looked from side to side then lifted the receiver from the wall telephone.

I couldn't make out the number she dialed, but whoever she called must've picked up on the first ring.

"I don't know what you're playing at," she said into the phone, "but I've paid you to do a job. You know what I expect. Tomorrow morning, on the beach. She's there every day." After a few seconds she replied, "Don't give me that crap. She'll want to go with you. I'll tell Nicholas she's run off. No need to worry over that one. I have plans for her, too, and they don't include you."

She slammed down the phone then seemed to remember she was supposed to be quiet, so she shushed the phone. After peering around again, she went back up the stairs.

I tucked my melted ice cream back inside the freezer. Was that Jack on the other end of the call Jingle made? Mrs. North was right, he had come back for her, and Jingle was involved, but why take me to dinner? How did I fit into the plan?

If I understood what Jingle was saying, she was paying Jack to kidnap Mrs. North and would somehow manipulate her into believing she was in love with Jack. How was I going to stop her?

Chapter 6

"I have an idea," I said as Mrs. North gathered her notebooks and pencils from the desk. "Let's drive down to Cape Henlopen for the day. We can pick up coffees and sandwiches on the way. And there's this great jazz musician you've got to hear. I downloaded his latest recording." I tried to shove earbuds at her. "Give it a listen."

"Cape Henlopen? What on earth for? We can walk twenty steps to our own beach. Besides, aren't there things you want to get done for our holiday weekend?"

"I think we need a change of scenery." I pasted a smile on my face, but I really wanted to yell, *"Stay away from your crazy mother-in-law, she wants to kidnap you!"* Instead, I said, "I thought you might like a little break from Jingle."

"Natalie, you know I never deviate from our schedule. It helps us stay on task. Changing our day will bring about confusion and we won't accomplish what needs to be completed."

"But, just this once, couldn't we go someplace different? Everything else will be the same."

"Is this about Jack? Will he be there? Are you planning to accidentally run into him?"

"No, no, anything but that. I heard what you said, and you're right. I'm staying away from him, far, far away. And you should, too."

"Why would I be anywhere near him?" Mrs. North asked.

"No reason. Just, you know, in the future. Stay away from him. I will, too." This was not going as planned. I'd slept poorly, if at all, and had barely a sip of coffee before Mrs. North was on the move.

"No dawdling, darling. Things to do, people to see." Mrs. North put on her hat and veil.

I hurried to keep pace with her. Grabbing the beach bag and her chair, I struggled to follow. Jingle had not come down yet, as she usually slept in until breakfast time and was uninterested in watching the sunrise.

Mrs. North stopped short, and I plowed into her back.

"Ouch. Why did you stop?" I asked, then glanced around her. The beach was swarming with police, lifeguards and medics. "What's happening?"

"Ma'am, the beach is closed right now," said an officer as he approached us. "There's been an accident."

"Accident?" said Mrs. North.

"Yes, a surfer. Looks like he collided with a boat of some sort. Search and Rescue are out there now hoping to recover the body."

Across the sand I saw a mangled surfboard. Not just any surfboard—the one that belonged to Nico.

"Let's go back to the house," I said, grabbing hold of Mrs. North's arms, hoping I could turn her away before she saw the surfboard herself.

"Officer, my husband surfs here every morning," said Mrs. North, but before he could reply, a lifeguard called him.

The officer left us and went down to the beach where a group of rescue workers gathered. They'd found the surfer.

"Please, let's go home," I said again, but she wouldn't budge, her eyes steady on what was left of Nico's surfboard.

"No, I won't leave here until I see him," she said.

"I'll go. Let me go. It's not him, but I'll check. I'll ask. We can't see anything from here. I bet Nico is over there helping."

Mrs. North nodded at me, but I doubted she heard any words I said. I eased her gently down on the sand before running toward the crowd.

"Hey, you! Lady, you can't come over here," said a young man in a white lifeguard tee shirt.

"I want to speak to the officer in charge," I said.

"He's busy," the young man said and turned away.

I was tired of being invisible and ignored. I went around him to where three men in wetsuits stood talking while a medic examined the body of a white-haired man in a tight black wetsuit.

"This man could be my boss," I said, and everyone looked at me.

The officer who spoke took my arm and turned me away from the body.

43

"Look, I know you're just doing your job, but this is mine. I'm their personal assistant. His wife is sitting over there," I said pointing toward Mrs. North who was now laying on the sand. "I don't want her to have to identify him. I can do it. Please, let me do it."

The officer sighed but nodded his head. "Okay, if you're sure. He wasn't in the water too long, but he was obviously hit by something. We think it was a boat. He has a few abrasions, but nothing that has disfigured his face."

I took a step and the officer grabbed hold of my arm.

"I'm okay," I said and realized I was crying.

He stayed right next to me, holding on, as we made our way past the others to the body on the beach.

Shutting my eyes, I took a deep breath and counted to five to steady myself. I looked at the wetsuit first. It was black and form-fitting, but Nico always wore one that had a red stripe up the side. This was plain black.

I forced my eyes to the man's face. He was older with white hair and a white beard, but he wasn't Nico.

"It's not him. That's not my boss." I tried not to sound so happy. After all, this man belonged to someone.

"You're positive it's not him?" asked the officer.

"I am absolutely positively sure he is not Nico, um, Mr. North."

"Okay then, I'm sure you and your boss are relieved," the officer said.

"There is one thing, though. The battered surfboard does belong to my boss."

"You sure?"

"Yes. He had them specially designed and built. That board is his."

The officer looked concerned and called over to one of the rescue workers. "We could be looking for a second body," he told the man.

My moment of happiness was quickly fading. Where was Nico?

By the afternoon no additional body had been found and Nico had been missing for at least twelve hours. I was making tea for Jingle, who refused to leave her room, but her sobs echoed through the house.

Mrs. North remained stoic. "He'll turn up, I'm positive," she said every time I went into the office to check on her. "See this ring?" she asked when I brought her coffee after delivering yet another cup of tea to Jingle. She held up the emerald-cut yellow diamond she wore on her left ring finger.

"It's gorgeous," I said. "Yours is the only yellow diamond I've ever seen."

"It isn't yellow; it's glowing. As long as it glows, I know my Nico is alive. We must find him."

I held her hand to get a closer look, and indeed the color seemed to be pulsing like a heartbeat. "What can we do? They have rescue teams searching the water now. Do you want to hire a boat?"

The doorbell interrupted our conversation.

"Stay here. I'll see who's there."

"You know I'm not to be disturbed, darling, no matter who it might be."

But Violet Doolittle was not going to be kept from her sister. "How is she, dearie?" Violet asked, marching directly past me and down the hall toward the office.

"She really doesn't want to see anyone, Mrs. Doolittle." I was getting a little tired of people pushing past me at the front door.

"I'm not anyone, I'm her sister. She needs me." She flung open the door and pulled Mrs. North into a hug.

"Violet, you're suffocating me." Mrs. North's voice was muffled, her face pressed tightly against Mrs. Doolittle's ample bosom.

"I just now heard. Poor, dear Nico. What will happen at Christmas? Who will take his place?"

"Violet, let go of me," Mrs. North said and gave her sister a gentle shove. She patted her hair back in place. "Nico will be fine by Christmas."

Mrs. Doolittle looked at me then at Mrs. North. "Dearie, I'm not here to upset you. I want to help, but the Coast Guard is searching for him as we speak. I've seen his surfboard lying on the beach. Police are everywhere. Why, I had no idea how many officers we had in this town. I don't think Nico will be here for Christmas."

Mrs. North's response was to point at her ring.

"My, now that does make a difference," Mrs. Doolittle said. "But surely, if he was able, he'd be here right now."

If he was able. If he was able. Those words caused a ringing in my ear. What if Nico was alright, but unable to get home? What had Jingle said on the phone last night? *Tomorrow morning on the beach*, that's what she said. I left the sisters and ran up the stairs to Jingle's room. I knocked four times before she answered.

"Go away," she called out.

"I will not leave until I see you. I want to make sure you're okay." I looked down at the teacups lined against the wall. She hadn't drank anything. "Open this door Jingle, or I'll break it down."

"You wouldn't," she said.

That was true, but she didn't know that for sure. "One, two," I counted.

"Hold your horses," she said. I could hear her shuffle to the door and turn the lock. "Happy? I'm as fine as I'm going to be right now. Oh, my baby. My poor baby boy." Jingle then collapsed in tears on her bed.

Whatever Jingle had planned, it didn't involve Nico being hurt or kidnapped. The woman was genuinely distraught. I sat next to her and placed my hand on her back. "It's going to be okay. Mrs. North feels certain he'll be coming home."

"Mrs. North does, does she?" Jingle pulled herself up and rested against the headboard. "You know that's not her married name, don't you? What's wrong with Kringle? How come she doesn't use that one? What married lady who loves her husband doesn't use his last name? Tell me?" Jingle crossed her arms.

"My understanding is that she wanted them to have a peaceful life here. Using her maiden name would draw less attention than Kringle would. You should come downstairs and eat something. You haven't had a single sip to drink and you're going to be dehydrated with all that crying."

Jingle shook her head and sniffled.

"Alright then, how about if I bring you something to eat here in your room? Would you like that?"

To this idea she nodded.

"I'll be back in a few minutes. Leave the door unlocked."

"I need ice cream," she said as I was shutting the door. Walking to the kitchen it occurred to me how much Jingle and Lady M were alike.

I took my coffee fudge ice cream and a pitcher of sweet tea with mint to Jingle then went to check if Mrs. North or Mrs. Doolittle needed anything before sneaking out. There was one person I thought might know what was going on.

Jack was sitting at the bar in Jam watching the Orioles game. I hopped on the stool next to his.

"What would you like?" Jack asked. "Should I order more champagne?"

"No, I can't stay," I said and was truly sorry. "You may not have heard what's been happening here today."

"Yes, they were just talking about it," Jack said and gestured to the two bartenders. "They said a man had been hit by a speedboat."

"That's true. Did they say they're also looking for another man?"

"No, I haven't heard that."

"Jack, Nico has gone missing. His surfboard was found nearly destroyed."

"That's horrible," Jack said. His expression remained the same, but I noticed his pupils dilated. "I'm very sorry to hear that, but even more sorry that we won't be spending the evening together."

"I'm afraid not," I said.

"It turns out I will be leaving town in the morning, but I hope to see you again the next time I'm here."

"I'd like that," I said as I stood. "And I'll offer your best wishes to Mrs. North and Jingle."

"Better not," Jack said clutching my wrist. "It's best that Jingle thinks I left town yesterday, and Bee, well, I'm sure she'd rather not hear from me at all." He released my arm. "Take care of yourself, Talia."

I smiled, nodded, and headed out the door to Baltimore Street. Then I slipped into the shadows and waited.

I wasn't sure what I intended to do. I could see his silver Jaguar from where I hid. How could I follow him on foot? I needed to call Mrs. North.

"Bring the car to Jam on Baltimore Street," I whispered into the phone. "I'll explain everything when you get here, but hurry."

I had hesitated too long. Before I could disconnect the call, Jack was in his car and driving off.

Chapter 7

"You're sure he hasn't hurt you?" Mrs. North asked for the fourth time.

I sat in the passenger seat of her forever dusty 1962 blue and white Mk1 Cortina. "No, it's nothing like that," I said and wished I'd told her everything I knew to begin with. We could have been following Jack right now. "I think Jack had Nico kidnapped."

Mrs. North gripped the steering wheel. "Why would you think that?" she asked after a long silence.

This was the part of the story I dreaded the most, telling Mrs. North about Jingle's involvement. I believed Mrs. North was capable of anything, both good and not so good when the situation called for it, and I was afraid of how she'd react.

I took a deep breath and plunged in. "The truth is I overheard Jingle on the phone last night. I believe she was talking to Jack and together they were plotting to kidnap you. How it ended up being Nico I couldn't say."

The steering wheel was gripped tighter, and Mrs. North's knuckles became whiter than usual. I could see every single vein. She sat so still I feared she'd stop breathing.

"What I can figure out is both Jingle and Jack seem shocked that Nico is the one missing. Obviously other people are involved. Jack said he's leaving town and that I'm not to mention him to you or Jingle. Whether this means he's washing his hands of the mess and cutting ties, or he's gone to see what's happened, I don't know."

"But you saw him this evening?"

"Yes, at Jam. We agreed to meet here at eight. I had no way of contacting him to cancel so I came to see what he knew."

"Have you discussed this with him?"

"Only that I couldn't stay because Nico was missing. Jack has no idea I'm on to him."

"When I find that Jack Frost," Mrs. North slammed both hands against the steering wheel hard enough that my hands stung. "He creates trouble wherever he goes, and together with Jingle, well, I tell you, darling, that is an unholy pair."

"Wait... did you say *Jack Frost*? You mean as in Jack Frost, old man winter?"

Mrs. North turned to me and blinked. "Of course, darling. Didn't you realize that?"

"No. Why would I?"

"After the things you've learned about me and Nico, and hearing Jack was from the North Pole as well, I assumed you knew that he was, um, different, too."

"Sister Margaret Mary always said to never assume. It makes an..."

"...ass of you and me, yes, I know," Mrs. North completed the cliche. "I tried to explain to you. He's not a person like Nico and me, or even the horrid Jingle. He's weather."

"I don't understand what you're saying."

"When a situation arises, he inhabits the body of a mortal. He chooses men who look similar, always average height, blond or silver-haired, and uses them for as long as needed. Growing up, I'd no idea about how he and his family worked. They found a family they liked and simply took them over. This is why I ended my relationship with him. Well, that and I'd met Nico. I found Jack and his family to be creepy," she said with a shiver.

"How will we find him again if he can body hop like that?" I asked.

"I think it's more difficult for him than that, and he doesn't exactly like change. If he's found a human he's comfortable in, he's likely to stay with him. Now, let's get back to the house and have a chat with my dear mother-in-law."

Mrs. North's words were filled with more ice than any of Jack's drinks.

The lights were off in Jingle's room. We sat in the car staring up at her window. "What are you going to say?" I asked Mrs. North.

"Say? I'm going to throttle her."

"I'm not sure that will help us find Nico. However, I have a plan."

"Do tell, darling, I'm all ears."

"What if I talk to Jingle and you listen in? You can read her mind, right? You'll know if she has information she's not sharing with me."

"It's not always that simple. I mean, why didn't I know what she was up to before now?"

"It isn't your fault. You've spent the last couple of days avoiding her most of the time. When you were around her, she wasn't necessarily thinking about kidnapping you."

"True." Mrs. North shrugged. "I should have watched her more closely. I know the mischief she's capable of causing. Poor Nico, he tries so hard to please her. I'm always surprised he married me. I'm the one thing he never gave in to her about." My employer turned the ring on her finger. Its glow illuminated her face. "I'm ready. We will give your idea a try."

Five minutes later I was tapping on Jingle's door. When there was no answer, I worried she may have skipped town along with Jack.

"Jingle?" I said quietly as I crept into her room. She lay in bed, her mouth wide open, gentle snores escaping her. "Jingle, wake up."

Turning on the bedside lamp, I found a bottle of sleeping pills. After a moment of panic, I realized the bottle was nearly full.

"Jingle, you need to wake up," I said as I shook her arm. "It's about Nico."

"Hmm, what?" Jingle opened one eye then the other. "What do you want?"

"It's Nico. Hurry, you need to get dressed. Someone's kidnapped him and they've made some rather peculiar demands."

"Kidnapped Nicholas? Who would do such a thing? Oh, my sweet boy." Jingle began to sob again.

"Who?" I asked Jingle but she only shook her head. "You wouldn't have any ideas, would you?"

"Ask that horrible sister of Beira's. Wasn't it only a few months ago that Doolittle dame was involved in a plot against Bee and my Nicholas? She's behind this as well, I'm sure."

"The man on the phone just now implied you were the person who knew what this was all about."

"Me? How dare you! Why would I ever put my son in harm's way? Get out, get out of here," she ordered. "When Nicholas returns—which I'm positive he will—I'll tell him the things you've said to me, the things you've implied."

"Go right ahead. I have plenty to tell him about a certain phone call you made during the middle of the night to Jack Frost."

"You little spy," Jingle said, her face nearly purple with rage. "That had nothing to do with my Nicholas."

"Didn't end up that way, though, did it?" I said as I walked from her room.

I must admit, at that moment, I was a bit afraid of turning my back on her.

Mrs. North and I tiptoed to her bedroom. Once safely inside I asked, "Did you get anything?"

"I am sorry to say it was hard to get through all that AquaNet she has shellacked over her hair. Once through, that woman's mind is filled mostly with dollar signs, caramel candy apples, and Tom Selleck dressed as the Marlboro Man." Mrs. North slumped on her bed. "Oh, and she thought of strangling you once or twice."

"Great. I'll lock my bedroom door tonight."

"We're no closer to finding Nico than we were earlier. I don't know what to do next," said Mrs. North. She gazed at Nico's side of the bed and took his pillow. Clutching it, she did something I thought impossible. Mrs. North cried.

"No, no, don't do that. We'll find him. In the morning you'll have an excellent plan, and I'll hate it, but I'll go along with it anyway, and in the end, Nico will be rescued. Okay?"

"I'm not sure things will work out that way this time," Mrs. North said, sniffling into Nico's pillow. "Maybe I'm not as clever as I thought."

This was far worse than the crying. A defeated Mrs. North was unimaginable.

"You are clever, you're brilliant, you're just sad right now. It will all come together. Let's sleep on it. Rest, it's all you need. Maybe a cigarette. What do you think?"

"I've no taste for one now." She fell back in the bed and curled up around the pillow.

I wasn't about to leave her in this state, so I did the only thing I knew. I lay next to her and held her until we both faded into sleep.

Chapter 8

The pounding on the front door came at nine the next morning. It took me a minute or two to realize where I'd fallen asleep.

Mrs. North stirred next to me, still clutching the pillow. I bolted from the bed and down the stairs hoping I'd get there in time before the noise woke her.

"What? What is it?" I asked, opening the door.

It was the man who'd cut in line getting coffee. He wore a light gray suit and stood on the step next to the police officer I'd spoken to yesterday morning. Had it all happened only yesterday?

"Mrs. North?" Mr. Rude asked.

"No, she's the assistant I told you about," said the officer. He gave me a shy smile. "Good morning, ma'am."

Calling me "ma'am" is never a good way to start off with me. Neither is coming between me and my coffee order. At that moment I let it go because he was obviously a detective and the police never showed up at your door early in the morning for no reason. They must have some word about Nico.

"Come in," I said, and led them into the kitchen.

"You are?" the suited man asked me.

"Natalie. I'm Natalie Tannon, personal assistant to Mrs. North."

"I'm Detective Nettles and this is Officer Anders. Is Mrs. North at home?"

"Yes, let me get her." I left the room, turning back once to find Detective Nettles watching me. There was no sign of recognition on his face. I'm sure I'm not the only person he's been rude to, so I couldn't expect him to remember me.

Before I made it halfway up the stairs, Mrs. North appeared. She was dressed in what she mistakenly believed was the current fashion. She wore her favorite candy cane striped blouse and red pencil skirt with a strand of pearls that would make June Cleaver envious. Basically, Mrs. North dressed like a woman who'd escaped from a 1950's comedy.

"The police are downstairs," I said as she passed me.

"Have they said anything about Nico?"

"Not to me. Not yet." I followed her through the living room and into the kitchen where the two men waited.

"Good morning, gentlemen," said Mrs. North. She sat in the chair closest to the window and they sat across from her after introducing themselves.

I made the coffee and unfortunately caught a glimpse of myself in the reflection of the toaster. My hair was smashed down on my head to one side. The other part was in a mass of tangles and unbrushed curls. Great. No doubt I'd be memorable now.

"Mrs. North, have you heard anything from your husband?" asked Detective Nettles. Officer Anders retrieved a small notebook from his pocket and began taking notes.

"Not a word, Detective. I just don't understand it." Mrs. North began to drum her fingers on the table, a sign that she needed a cigarette, but she never smoked in front of strangers.

I rushed over with her coffee, hoping that would calm her nerves.

"We've covered a lot of ground. Divers spent hours searching, but we've come up empty. Is it possible he never went surfing? Maybe he gave his board to the man we found," Detective Nettles said. "Or maybe he has reason for wanting you to believe he's dead."

"That's impossible." I handed both men a cup of coffee. "Officer Nettles, he would never, ever leave here like that. Ever."

"*Detective* Nettles," he corrected me.

I was working out a snide response, but before I could form it, Mrs. North spoke up.

"Suppose someone took him," she said, holding her mug between her hands.

"Why would you think that has happened? Has someone contacted you asking for ransom?" Detective Nettles asked.

Officer Anders stopped writing and both men stared at us.

What would Mrs. North say? Would she tell them about Jingle and her plot to abduct Mrs. North? I held my breath.

"No one has contacted me. Yet. But it has occurred to me that these things happen. I write a column, as you must be aware, and maybe I've given bad advice or hurt someone's feelings. I have run many scenarios through my mind."

"You believe your husband may have been kidnapped due to something you've written?" asked the detective.

Mrs. North nodded her response.

"What about him? He has no enemies, no one who might hold a grudge? What does your husband do for a living, Mrs. North?"

Mrs. North paused and glanced at me. "For the most part, Nico is retired. His family owns a toy making business up north. We don't go there often anymore. There are others who see to the operations. Nico mostly spends his time surfing, meditating, practicing yoga, and riding his motorcycle."

"Everyone loves him," I said, finding myself near tears. "No one, absolutely no one would ever want to hurt him."

"But someone would want to hurt you?" Detective Nettles kept his eyes on Mrs. North.

"As I've said, I have no known enemies, but it is possible I've hurt or offended someone in my column."

"Do you have a recent photo of your husband, Mrs. North?" asked Officer Anders.

"I'll get you one," I said, grateful for the chance to leave the room. I could feel tears beginning to fall. While Mrs. North sat emotionless, I was a quivering mess. It would definitely leave the wrong impression with the police.

As I brought the photo back into the kitchen, a crash came from above. Jingle had risen.

"Is there someone else in the house?" asked Detective Nettles.

Mrs. North and I exchanged a look that wasn't missed by the detective who arched his brow.

"It's only..." Mrs. North and I said at once.

Jingle appeared before we could say another word.

"Good morning, boys," she greeted them, sashaying in wearing a tight pink negligee and a feather boa.

"Gentlemen, may I introduce to you my mother-in-law, Jingle... North," said Mrs. North, cringing.

Jingle did not appear pleased with her new surname.

"Who needs more coffee?" I said, and refilled all the cups.

"Honey, what's your name?" Jingle asked, squeezing in between the detective and the officer.

"Me? Anders, ma'am," said the young officer, hot red dots forming on both his cheeks.

Detective Nettles seemed to pick up on the fact that something was odd about Jingle. Just in case, when he looked my way, I nodded in her direction and twirled my finger near the side of my head to indicate she was cuckoo.

"We won't trouble you further right now," said Detective Nettles standing. "It would be helpful if you came down to the station, though, and we could talk more."

"I'll come, too," said Jingle. "I just love men in uniforms."

Officer Anders couldn't get out of the kitchen fast enough. I walked them to the door. Detective Nettles hung back as the officer walked to their car.

"Ms. Tannon, about the other morning. I'm sorry. I was quite rude. Not that it's an excuse, but my team was in the midst of a big case and I was anxious to get back."

"So, you're new at this detective thing," I said.

"I am. How'd you know that?"

"The new guy buys the coffees."

"Right. Okay, see you at the station later," he said and went to the car.

I shut the door. Maybe he wasn't such a rude guy after all.

Chapter 9

"Times up, old lady." Mrs. North had her sharp nailed finger pointed in Jingle's face. "We know what you planned and how it's all gone wrong. Tell us now where to find Nico, or you're going to the police station with us, and you won't be returning here."

I was impressed. All those reruns of *Cagney and Lacey* had given Mrs. North ample material and she imitated Sharon Gless perfectly. Even I was intimidated.

"You know, honey, I'd almost believe you, if I didn't know all your secrets." Jingle laughed as she swatted Mrs. North away and took her compact from her flimsy robe to check her hair.

"My secrets are your secrets, but even if it means exposing our true identities to the world, I will stop at nothing to find Nico."

"How many times do I need to say that I'm not a part of any kidnapping plot? No matter what you believe me to be, you know I could never put my boy in harm's way."

Jingle folded over a curl between her fingers. Her hairspray was always close at hand. We would need to have the air quality of the house checked once she was gone.

"Jingle, I heard you on the phone, and I wasn't spying, I was... I was eating ice cream."

"Natalie, what have I told you about eating late at night?" Mrs. North let out a disappointed sigh. "Your digestive system, especially your liver, needs a rest. And ice cream? All that dairy is hard enough on your system without indulging after dinner."

"I know. I know, but could we get back to the point? Jingle, I heard you on the phone talking to Jack. He was to meet Mrs. North on the beach and take her away. That never happened. I believe you have no idea where Nico might be, but you can't deny your involvement with Jack. He told me all about you." It was my turn to cross my arms. Maybe I was Tyne Daily now.

"Okay, you got me." Jingle held her comb up like a flag in surrender. "I saw Jack a few weeks back. He was pretty dashing in his new, let's just say threads. You know what I mean? It occurred to me he'd chosen a man similar to my Nicholas. Jack's always been jealous of my boy," Jingle said, turning toward me. "It was more than just over you, Miss Thing," she said, turning her attention back on Mrs. North. "What either of them find so attractive about you is lost on me. Anyway, seeing him gave me the idea. You know you loved Jack once. You would've married him had you not discovered how the Frosts kept their family together, so to speak."

"I would never have married him. Once I met Nico there was no one in the world but him for me." Mrs. North's eyes glistened with tears.

I really couldn't take the crying—from either of them—anymore. "So then what? You met Jack in his new skin and got this genius idea. Go on."

"I'd put in Beira's mind that it was Jack she really wanted. She'd go off happily with him, Nicholas would be free, and he could be with you, who in my opinion is a more suitable Mrs. Claus."

"You're just like your father," said Mrs. North, sitting heavily into the chair Detective Nettles had vacated.

"I am not. I've never even met the old so and so. You take that back," said Jingle, putting her comb down and reaching for her hair spray.

"I will not. The truth hurts." Mrs. North snatched the Aqua Net away from her mother-in-law.

"Ladies," I said, stepping closer to the table. "None of that matters now. We need to find out where Nico is, and the first step will be to contact Jack. How do we do that?"

"I don't know," Jingle claimed.

"You called him," I said.

"True, but if he's left the house where he was staying, I'd have no other number for him."

"We must start someplace. Give it a try." Mrs. North handed the phone to Jingle.

She snatched it out of Mrs. North's hand and pressed the numbers carefully as if she was cracking a safe. "Jack?" Jingle said into the receiver. "Oh, sorry, honey. Must have the wrong number."

The kitchen was silent. Our only lead gone. There was nothing else to do except...

"I am going to tell the police everything." Mrs. North picked up her veiled hat and headed for the door.

"What do you mean 'Tell the police everything'?" I said, barely scrambling into the passenger seat before Mrs. North pulled away from the curb.

"I'm positive they will believe I'm out of my mind, but it's a chance I have to take. We need their help in locating Nico."

"Suppose we say we received an anonymous tip," I said.

"I'm afraid that won't work, darling. They would surely check our phone records."

"We could say it came in a letter. A letter that dissolved after we read it." Sounded plausible to me.

"No, all we have is the truth. That's what I'll stick with."

We drove the rest of the way in silence.

Ten minutes later we were walking into the Rehoboth Police Station. A few officers passed by us and gave Mrs. North a quizzical glance, but I'm sure it wasn't often they were visited by a woman wearing a white veil who wasn't a bride. Probably not many brides visited the station, come to think of it.

"Good afternoon, I'm Mrs. North and I would like to speak to Detective Nettles."

The desk sergeant looked us over. "Okay. Take a seat over there on the bench. He'll be right with you."

We sat side by side. I was extremely nervous, my legs jiggling around until Mrs. North clenched her teeth and told me to be still.

Within minutes Detective Nettles emerged down the hallway with a young woman. She wiped her face with a tissue and nodded as he spoke quietly to her. They shook hands then she left.

"Mikey, two women over there to see you. Quite the ladies' man today, aren't you?" the sergeant snickered, but the detective ducked his head as if he'd been physically struck.

"Mrs. North, Ms. Tannon, if you'll both follow me."

We walked in the same direction from which he came. He led us to a small office and we each took a seat around his desk. I noted how tidy it was, but mostly it was the photograph he had on his blotter that drew my attention.

"I know that man," I blurted out.

"This man? The one in the picture?" Detective Nettles looked at me then at Mrs. North. "Do you know him as well?"

"I do not," she said. "But he bears a striking resemblance to my husband."

"Ms. Tannon, you're not confusing him with your employer?" the detective asked me.

"Of course not. I obviously know my employer's own husband."

"Of course. Could you tell me how you know this man?"

This was going to be tricky. "We went out to dinner. It was two nights ago, I think."

"You think?"

"Look, a lot's happened over the past couple of days. I feel like I've lived a week since then."

"Fair enough." Detective Nettles picked the photograph up from his desk. "Could you tell me where you went and some of the things you talked about. Did he seem upset, preoccupied, nervous?"

"He took me to La Fable. I did most of the talking. It was our first date. He asked me general things, you know, stuff about where I was from, what I did for a living, that sort of thing."

"How did you meet?" the detective wanted to know.

This was going to take some thought. "You see, well..."

"Was it on some online dating service," Detective Nettles said, his face pinched as if he smelled rotten fish.

"No, it was not some online dating service," I said, maybe yelled, just a little. Lowering my voice, I continued. "I met him at the house. Mrs. North's house, I mean." I glanced at her. "He had the wrong address and we got to talking. That's how he came to ask me out." I leaned my back against the chair. My hands were shaking.

"That's interesting, but helpful. The woman who just left here is Mr. Hayden's wife."

"Who is Mr. Hayden?" I asked.

"The man in the picture. He must have told you his name. Right?"

"That wasn't the name he used."

Detective Nettles grabbed a pen from a cup. "What name did he give you?"

Could I really say this? "Jack. He said his name was Jack."

"Just Jack? No last name?"

"Okay, he said his name was Jack Frost."

Detective Nettles put his pen down and looked at his desk. I could see he was trying not to smile. "Jack Frost, is that right?" He nodded at me with something like pity in his eyes.

I focused on the framed diploma above his head. "Yep. Jack Frost. I fell for that one."

Detective Nettles shrugged. "Anyway, Mrs. Hayden reported him missing. Told her he was going out to meet a client for a drink last night and never returned home. She said he's been acting secretive this week, but if he was having an affair with you, that would explain his behavior."

"I was not having an affair with this man. We had one dinner, that was all." Then I recalled our kiss and could feel my face flare.

"Don't forget you met him for drinks, darling," Mrs. North helpfully pointed out.

"When was this?" The detective retrieved his pen and started writing.

I glared at Mrs. North before answering, "Last night."

"What's that?" I once again had Detective Nettles's full attention.

"I said last night. I met this man, known to me as Jack Frost, last night around eight at Jam on Baltimore Street for a drink. I didn't have one, though. I told him my boss was missing and I couldn't stay. He said that was too bad, then I left. I was still standing outside when minutes later he came out and drove away in a Jaguar."

"Why were you still outside if you couldn't stay for a drink?" He put the pen on his desk again. "Were you waiting for him to come out?"

"No, why would I? I called Mrs. North to ask if she wanted anything while I was still out. I'm trying to tell you what I know about him and when I last saw him, that's all."

"Okay. Noted. You have been helpful and what you said corroborates with what Mrs. Hayden reported."

"I didn't know he was married."

"Should I put that in my report?" Detective Nettles gave me a thin smile.

I shook my head. Figures, another married man.

Mrs. North held my hand. "It's alright, Natalie. Detective, could we please move on and discuss why we are here? Unless you need any additional help with your other cases that is..."

"No, you're right. Thank you, Natalie, I mean Ms. Tannon, for your help. As for Mr. North, I'm sorry to report we have not been able to locate him. However, a group of young men have come forward and reported that the man found in the water is known as 'Hey Man.' He frequents the beach and is believed to be homeless. They also told us another older man, who we believe to be your husband," he said nodding at Mrs. North, "is often seen talking with him and giving him money. We're now working on two theories. The first being that your husband gave Hey Man his surfboard, and being an inexperienced surfer, he was killed in the accident."

"That doesn't explain what happened to my husband."

"No, it doesn't. But our second theory does. I've thought about your concern of kidnapping. What if your husband was not taken because of anything you wrote, but was mistaken for Hey Man? We can't find any criminal record from Hey Man's fingerprints, we don't even have his legal name, but that doesn't mean he wasn't caught up with some unsavory situations. We haven't found anyone connected with him or even where he spent his time when away from the beach."

"Are you saying you now agree with me that my husband is being held against his will?"

Detective Nettles nodded. "It's one possibility."

Mrs. North left the car parked in front of the station. "I need to walk to think. Oh, Natalie, this has become so much more complicated and darker than I could have imagined."

I walked along silently beside her. My father always said things were usually simple, but we made them complicated. I didn't believe Nico had been mistaken for Hey Man. All the answers were with Jack—or Mr. Hayden, or whatever his name was.

When we find him, we'll find Nico. I felt sure of this.

Chapter 10

The front door to the Doolittle Boarding House stood ajar. I called out, but no one answered. Mrs. North followed me into the house. Pangs of homesickness for this place still occasionally crept up on me. I traced my finger along the hall table and ran my hand over the fringe that hung from the lamp shade. Mrs. Doolittle's was my idea of the perfect family home.

"I thought I heard someone come in," said Mrs. Doolittle, wiping her hands on her ruffled apron. "Come on back, dearies, I've just heated the kettle."

Standing next to each other, it was hard to believe the tall, sleek Mrs. North was the older sister of the petite and curvy Mrs. Doolittle. They had grown up in the North Pole, but sisterly competition had fractured their once close relationship. That was mostly mended after I came to work for Mrs. North.

"You know, Bee, this is the first time you've come to call on me," said Mrs. Doolittle.

"You've never invited me, Violet," said Mrs. North, accepting a cup of tea.

"Natalie, I've made your favorite—chocolate scones. I had a feeling you might drop in today."

Mrs. North chose a scone from the plate. "Are these gluten-free?"

"For heaven sakes, Bee, just eat it. You don't have any allergies. Now tell me what's happened. Has Nico been found?"

Between bites—well, if I'm being totally honest it was between my second and third scone—I caught Mrs. Doolittle up on what was happening. She listened attentively, pushing the plate of scones toward me.

"I really can't eat another," I said.

"You really shouldn't," added Mrs. North. "That's a lot of sugar, probably more than the recommended serving for a few days."

Mrs. Doolittle rolled her eyes but didn't comment. "This Mr. Hayden fellow. I'm positive we've done some work for him." She eased off her chair and went to the office, returning seconds later with her notebook.

"What do you have there?" Mrs. North asked.

"This is how I keep track of the jobs I take on." She turned the page and ran her finger down each line. "Yes, here it is. I knew that name sounded familiar. Dale Hayden requested a temp for his office. He needed a receptionist. I sent Penny to help him."

"Penny?"

"The new girl," said Mrs. Doolittle.

"Oh, right. What's-her-name." I laughed. "I promise I'll remember to call her Penny from now on."

"When did she work for him?" Mrs. North asked.

"Last week, for about three days. She's over working the counter at Dolle's today until closing if you need to talk to her."

"That might be a good idea," said Mrs. North. "We need to find him. Natalie's convinced if we find him, we will find Nico." Again Mrs. North touched her ring which still glowed brightly.

"He'll be back, Bee, don't you worry. Oh, that darn Jack Frost. He always looks so pretty... then before you know it, you're standing in a pile of dirty slush." Mrs. Doolittle rung her tea towel between her hands. "He better not cross my path."

We walked from Mrs. Doolittle's to Dolle's where Penny was helping one of my former favorite customers.

"Miss Hardy! How have you been?" I gave her a quick hug. I didn't want her to spill her coffee or her bag of toffee.

After a quick chat, while Mrs. North waited patiently beside me, I turned my attention to Penny.

"Can I help you?" she asked.

"I hope so," I said. "I was wondering if on your break we could talk for a few minutes."

"About what?"

"Mrs. Doolittle told us you did some temp work for a physical therapist office owned by a Mr. Dale Hayden."

"I did. What's this have to do with your Christmas candy order?" she asked Mrs. North.

"Nothing, darling, the order stands. This is an entirely different matter."

"Go on," said a young blonde girl behind the counter. "Take your break now while things are slow."

Penny came out from behind the counter and the three of us walked to The Mug and Spoon and ordered coffees. Mrs. North treated.

"How did you find working for Mr. Hayden?" I asked after taking a sip of my coffee.

"It was easy. He was never there. The first day he was all business, must've had at least seven patients come in. The next day he turned up and said to cancel all the appointments for the next two weeks. Said he was taking a vacation and if I needed anything he could be reached on his cell. Said he was going to relax on his boat."

"He has a boat?" Mrs. North asked.

"Yep, a big one. He has a painting of it in the reception area of his office."

"Tell me, Penny, have the police spoken to you?" I asked.

"The police? Why would they want to talk to me?"

"Mr. Hayden has gone missing. His wife reported it this morning." I blew my coffee before taking another sip. "Who is his regular receptionist?"

"Apparently, he married her. I was hoping that he'd offer me a permanent position there. It's not far and I liked the office, and he seemed easy-going, too. He said he was going to keep the position filled with temps for the time being. I was disappointed, but Mrs. Doolittle said that's common. She said it's cheaper to have temps to fill in than to hire a full-time receptionist. He'd have to pay sick leave and medical insurance in addition to wages."

"That could be true," Mrs. North agreed. "Now, Penny, would you happen to know where this boat is docked?"

"No, sorry, but if I remember correctly, he also had a photo of his boat in his office. I hope that helps whatever it is you two are doing."

"We'd appreciate it if you didn't repeat any of this to anyone," I said.

"Any of what?" Penny asked. Seemingly dazed, she walked back to Dolle's without ever giving us another glance.

"Good-bye, Penny," said Mrs. North and linked arms with me, pulling me up the street to the station to retrieve her car.

"Did you make her forget?" I asked Mrs. North once we were belted in. I saw Detective Nettle peering out at us from the window.

"It's much better for everyone if they stay a bit vague about things where I'm concerned."

"What about Detective Nettles? Does he remember talking to us?" I asked her.

"Of course, darling. We can't have him forgetting a thing until my Nico is found."

"Where to now?"

"To Hayden's office to get a look at that photo. We must find his boat," said Mrs. North, lighting a candy cane cigarette and turning up her Blondie CD.

It was barely a hop, skip, and jump to Hayden's office. We drove around the block three or four times, but there was no one about. Parking over on the next street we made our way to the back entrance.

"Are we going to break in?" Memories of our secret mission to the Everywhere Corporation filled my mind.

"No worries, Natalie. I've brought all the tools we will need." She pulled out a tension wrench and a flathead screwdriver. "These should do the trick."

"Wait a minute. Suppose he has an alarm? We should have thought to ask Penny," I said.

"You make a good point." Mrs. North put the tools back in her bag. "There's a window over there. If we push the garbage can over, you could slip through then let me in the door."

"Me? I'm not going to fit in that tiny space. I'd have to lose ten pounds at least. Why don't you go? You're much slimmer than I am."

"Darling, I'm simply not dressed for that type of activity. I can barely move my legs in this pencil skirt as it is."

"Fine," I huffed. "I'll try, but no pushing me in the window. If I can't make it, we'll just have to come up with a different plan. Agreed?"

Mrs. North said nothing.

"Do you agree? If not, I'm leaving now."

"Alright, already. I agree. Happy?"

Together we rolled the large trash can over until it was against the building directly under the window. From this angle, the space appeared even smaller. There was no way I was going to fit, but Mrs. North would never take my word for it. I'd need to prove it.

I hoisted myself on top of the can and grabbed hold of the windowsill.

"You're doing marvelous, darling," Mrs. North called from below. "Just another inch or two."

I pulled my body halfway in the window. Maybe I'd fit after all. I had been walking more. Then I remembered the coffee fudge ice cream and just like that I could feel my stomach bloat. I couldn't move forward or backward. My feet no longer reached the trash can lid. "I'm stuck."

"Hello there!" I heard Mrs. North say. A few minutes later she was standing in front of me.

"How did you get in?" I asked her as she tugged on my arms, nearly pulling them out of their sockets. "Just open the window wider, for Pete's sake."

"Good idea," she said before flipping the locks and yanking up the window frame.

I fell into the room with a thud. "That was graceful," I said, dusting my clothes off. I will never wear pants again when I go out with her. "Are you going to tell me how you got in?"

"He has a janitorial service. I told them I was Hedda Nelson, and I was with the Safety and Health of Workers Organization. I told them this window was a hazard and that you, my assistant, were checking it out. They are in the next office writing out their grievances now. We'll take their concerns to the board."

"What board?"

"I'll think about that later. Let's get a look at that photo before we run out of time."

Just as Mrs. North said, two women and a man sat in Mr. Hayden's office busily writing. The photo of the boat—a white and red cabin cruiser—sat on the corner of his desk. I discreetly snapped a shot of it with my phone.

"I'm sorry to interrupt you but we must move on to our next assignment," said Mrs. North as she collected all the papers. "Your concerns will be addressed."

They each thanked us and together walked us to the door. We hurried down the street to the car.

"You have a real problem," I said to her once we were on the road. "Those people might have serious concerns. What are we going to do with those lists?"

"Natalie, darling, I will take care of it. I will see to it that these lists find their way to the people who can help them. Isn't that what I do? People send me letters all the time telling me what they want and need, and I give it to them."

"Children send letters, and you deliver toys. That's different."

"Do you really think only children ask for things? When we find Nico I'll have him show you some of the letters he receives, and believe me, they're not all from children."

We were back in front of the police station. Mrs. North pulled the car into a parking space as I studied the picture of the boat on my phone. I made the photo larger so she could see, and we studied the background details. In the picture I recognized a building. I was sure this boat was docked at a marina in Dewey.

We drove down Route One to Dewey Beach, reaching the marina just as the sun set. The first thing I noticed was the silver Jaguar in the lot. We parked directly next to it.

"Now what?" I asked. "Hayden's here, or at least Jack is, but how do we find him?"

"We'll wait until it gets a bit darker, then have a look around. I feel sure Nico is here." She admired her ring that seemed to glow brighter.

A few people passed us, none of them Hayden, but they didn't seem to pay any attention to two middle-aged women. I was always surprised Mrs. North's car didn't attract some admirers, but no one ever gave it a second look.

We waited thirty minutes or so before getting out of the car. There was a slight breeze coming off the water. It was nice after the hot days we'd been experiencing.

Mrs. North smoothed down her skirt. I was worried she'd get her heels caught between the planks on the boardwalk. We walked up the pier. It was quiet around here, especially considering it was the week of the fourth of July.

"You head that way. I'll see what's down here." Mrs. North pointed behind her. "If you find anything—anything at all that seems out of place— call me." She walked a few steps before turning back. "And, darling, it goes without saying, call me if you see the boat."

"Will do, boss," I said and went off with my phone and a small flashlight.

I kept close to the boats, not walking out in the middle where I could be easily spotted. I hoped Mrs. North would be okay, as not many women were dressed like her, especially at the marina. Or anyplace in this century. I shook my head. She really needed to watch more current television programs.

I'd passed at least twenty-some boats before I spotted the red and white cruiser. It looked larger here than it had in the photo. From where I stood, I could see a gleam of light coming from below the deck.

I pressed Mrs. North's name on my phone. "I have our target in sight."

"Who is this?"

"Jingle? What are you doing here?" I whispered.

"Here? I'm in the house. Where are you? More importantly, where's my wayward daughter-in-law?" Then her voice changed from sour to sweet. "That nice police officer came back to see her. She should have been home waiting for her husband to return."

"We'll be home soon. Hopefully we'll be bringing Nico with us." No thanks to you, I wanted to add. "Why do you have Mrs. North's phone anyways?"

"She left it. You rang and I answered."

"Great. Goodbye." I hung up before she could say anything else.

The phone rang immediately, Mrs. North's name flashing on the screen. I ignored it. It was going to take forever to find my boss now. I retraced my steps then headed in the direction where I last saw her.

"Mrs. North," I whispered, but there was no reply. The pier was empty. "Mrs. North," I called slightly louder, still everything was quiet. Where could she be? She was probably looking for her phone. I should have made sure she had it with her before we split up. The only thing to do was to go back to the boat and hope she would eventually find it.

I quickened my pace as I headed toward the cruiser. Rounding the corner, I spotted two men standing on the deck smoking so I ducked behind a mooring. The men hadn't noticed me. Typical... after forty, most women became invisible.

I peeked around to check if they had gone. Neither man was Hayden. We were going to need back-up. Mrs. North and I couldn't subdue three grown men to rescue Nico. The smartest thing to do would be to contact Detective Nettles.

I heard my name being called as I pulled my phone from my pocket. The voice didn't belong to Mrs. North. I looked up to find Detective Nettles heading straight for me.

"Thank goodness I caught up with you. What are you doing out here?" he asked.

"I was going to call you. I think Nico, I mean Mr. North, is on that boat. Hayden's car is in the lot, so I expect he's there, too. Mrs. North is around here someplace, but I can't find her."

"Slow down," he said, putting his hands on my arms. His touch was cool.

"Detective Nettles?"

"It's me, Talia."

"Jack," I said and pulled away from him with such force my phone slipped from my hands. I grabbed for it but missed, then watched as it fell between the boats and into the water with barely a splash. "Crap. Look what you made me do."

"Hayden's on the boat," he said. "So is Nico, but it's not what you think. It is, but it isn't. I can explain all of this."

"Sure, it isn't strange at all," I mocked. "First, you're a silver-haired man with a neatly trimmed beard who owns a physical therapy group. Now you're a six-foot-two dark-haired detective. I'm sure it's easy to explain that."

"I knew you'd understand. Talia, from the moment I met you something changed inside of me. I wanted to make a go of it with Hayden's body since you really seemed attracted to him, but then his wife showed up. I swear, I had no idea the guy was married."

I crossed my arms. "Sure, that's what they all say."

"Please, let me try to tell you what happened. It's not my fault. That blasted Jingle—the woman's a menace. She had me convinced Bee was pining away for me, but meeting you broke whatever spell that big-haired woman put on me. I told her no way was I going off with Bee. She wouldn't listen. So I hired these guys to... you know, keep her occupied for a while. They're as dense as you would imagine. Instead, they snatched up Nico. I had no idea. The other guy who was helping them wound up dead. It's all a mess."

"You must be crazier than I think if you want me to believe all that horse manure," I said. "Now get on that boat and get Nico. Tell those guys the game's over."

"Okay, here's the thing. They have guns. They're also fed up with Hayden—well, me—but they think I'm Hayden. They have him tied up and stowed away in a closet. They're waiting for my wife, his wife... definitely his wife... to bring the ransom."

"What? Where's Nico?"

"Nico, he's another story. He's too nice. He has no idea he's been abducted. Those two got him on the boat by feeding him some story about how he's helping them find the dead guy's family. Nico hasn't even tried to escape. He doesn't know about Hayden being taken hostage. He thinks he went to get supplies. I tried my best to get him off the boat, honestly I did, but he wouldn't go. He thinks Bee is meeting him in Ocean City, which is where they've told him they're going."

I slapped my hand to my forehead. This was a complete mess. How could Nico be so gullible? We couldn't have any more of this nonsense.

"If you're going to jump into a police officer's body, then you better act like one. Get up there and arrest those creeps," I said, placing my hands on my hips to show I meant business.

"I'll do it," Jack finally said. "I'll do it for you." But he failed to move, only stood there like his feet were frozen on the dock.

"No, not for me. You'll do it because it's the right thing to do," I said, giving him a slight shove.

"There you are, darling." Mrs. North came down the dock like she was a top model on a runway.

"Good. You're here, too, Detective. We may need your assistance."

Jack looked at me with those crystal blue eyes I knew were his and not Detective Nettles and shook his head.

"Yes, Detective Nettles here was just about to radio for back-up. We have two men on board with weapons and two hostages. The detective has some inside information and has assured me Nico is unharmed. Isn't that right, Detective Nettles?"

"Ah, yes, yes, certainly is. And around here someplace I must have a car with a radio to alert my team. I have a car, right?" he asked me.

"Detective, are you alright? You seem out of sorts." Mrs. North gave me a questioning look.

"I think he had a bit of a fall while spying on the suspects," I said. "Let me help you to your car."

"You do that, Natalie. I'll just pop up and tell Nico to get his things together so we can go home."

"You can't just pop up. He's not on a playdate," I said.

"He sort of is," Jack said. "At least he thinks that it's an outing."

I rolled my eyes and turned to Mrs. North. "Did you not hear or understand what Ja... Detective Nettles told me? They have guns. You are a lot of magical things, but being indestructible is not one of them."

"You said Jack." Mrs. North glared past me at Detective Nettles.

"No, I didn't."

"Yes, you did." Mrs. North formed a fist and knocked on Detective Nettles's forehead. "Jack, are you in there?"

"Bee, knock it off."

"I'll knock you off." She rolled up her other fist and punched him in the eye.

"Holy bleeping cow, that hurt. What did you do that for?" asked Jack, holding his hand to his eye.

"With humanity comes pain," said Mrs. North, reeling back to sock him again.

"Break it up, you two," I said. A little too loudly, because now we'd drawn the attention of the two men on the boat... and Nico.

"Ahoy there, Bee," Nico waved from the deck of the boat.

"Nico," she said and rushed up the plank toward him. Mrs. North pushed right past those men and flung her arms around Nico's neck, pecking his cheek with kisses.

My heart was in my throat. What would they do now? Would they just release Nico?

"Everybody on the boat," the chubbier of the two men said, looking at me and Jack.

"We're leaving," said Mrs. North. "You boys have had enough fun. My Nico needs his rest."

"You're not going anywhere, lady. Sit down. You two, get up here now," he said, pointing a small pistol in our direction.

What could we do but comply? "Do you have a phone?" I whispered to Jack.

"I think so," he patted his pockets. "I'm going to hand it to you." Quickly he slid the phone into my hand before we reached the boat.

"Nine-one-one," I said quietly, trying not to move my lips. Thankfully the phone began to dial the number. They were bound to trace the call when no one spoke.

I followed Jack onto the boat and, using him as cover, slid the phone onto the cushion of a deck chair. I hoped the men wouldn't hear the voice of the operator when the call was picked up.

"What is the meaning of this?" Mrs. North asked. "My husband had a swell time, but now we need to leave."

Good. With her shrieking, no one would be able to hear when the operator came on.

"That's right," I added to the noise. "What's the meaning of holding us at gunpoint on this boat?"

"Why are you yelling?" asked the short man with the gun. "Sit down and button up."

"We are leaving now. Come along, Nico. Come along, Natalie."

"You're not leaving until we get paid," said the taller of the two. He was now holding a gun as well and pointing it directly at Detective Nettles. "Remember me, Nettles? Nice to know I helped you make detective."

"Sure," said Jack. "How've you been?"

"You want to know how I've been?" said Mr. Tall, and gave a laugh that made the hair on the back of my neck stand on end. "I just served seven years upstate."

"That's too bad." Jack gave him a pat on the shoulder.

"Shut up, Jack. Just shut up," I said.

"What did I say?" Jack asked innocently.

"Nico, why didn't you just tell me you wanted to go on a fishing trip with your little friends? I've been so worried." Mrs. North opened her purse. "How much does he owe you?"

What was wrong with her? She knew darn well these men were not here to entertain Nico. I raised my eyebrows as if to ask what was up, but then I saw how her eyes twinkled and braced myself for whatever she had planned.

"Do you have change? Maybe you'd like a check. I have a check," Mrs. North said, rooting through her purse.

Before they could answer, Mrs. North whipped out a can of Aqua Net. I immediately shut my eyes and threw my hand against Jack's face, accidentally knocking him off balance and sending him over the railing onto the pier.

Mrs. North wasted no time and sprayed the men—unfortunately including Nico—in the eyes with the hair spray.

While the men screamed and rubbed their hands over their faces, I rammed into the tall guy hard enough that he dropped his gun overboard and into the water below.

Mrs. North took on the smaller, rounder man, felling him with a kick in the family jewels. "No one keeps me from my Nico," she said before grinding the heel of her shoe into his plump thigh.

"Uncle, uncle," the round man cried out.

The man I'd hit was staggering around the deck. "I think I'm blind," he yelled.

I was relieved to hear sirens and see flashing lights enter the marina. I ran down to the dock.

Detective Nettles lay motionless. I kneeled beside him and put his head on my lap.

"Jack, Jack, wake up," I said.

His eyes fluttered open and brown eyes stared back at me. Jack was gone.

"Ms. Tannon?" Detective Nettles sat up slowly, holding the back of his head. "What's happened?"

"You fell. Well, actually I knocked you down."

Officer Anders came running toward us. "Sir, are you hurt?"

"I'll be fine, Anders."

"He needs to go to the hospital," I said. "He's had a bad fall and could have a concussion."

"Yes, ma'am," said Anders. "I'll radio for an ambulance. Anyone else get hurt?"

"No, but two men were sprayed in the eyes with Aqua Net, and there's a man tied up in a closet below decks."

"Aqua what? Was it some sort of water pistol?" Officer Anders wanted to know.

I laughed. "No, it's hair spray." I looked up at the deck where several officers were searching the boat and had handcuffed the two suspects. Mrs. North and Nico were nowhere to be seen.

Chapter 11

"You'll watch *It's a Wonderful Life* or you'll leave," Mrs. North told Jingle. "I'll have no more nonsense out of you. Natalie's worked hard to put this holiday together—a holiday you nearly ruined, I might add, and we are going to follow her plans to the letter. Understand?"

Jingle grumbled.

"What's that, you say?" Mrs. North asked.

"Not a thing. I know when to keep my mouth shut." Jingle slumped onto the chair next to Mrs. Doolittle.

"Now don't be that way, dearie. My sister did a good thing letting you stay on here. She's not usually so nice."

"I'm trying to be good," Jingle pouted. "Nico has asked me to give her a chance, and after all, she did save him from those hooligans. She's still upset with me though I've explained a million times it was all Jack's fault. She should be angry with him."

I set up the DVD and pulled down the screen. We were three minutes into the movie when the doorbell rang. And rang.

"I'll get it," I said. "Carry on without me. I've seen this one before."

I ran down the steps before the bell could be pushed again. Opening the door, I found Detective Nettles on the step.

"I'm sorry to interrupt your evening," he said. "There's just a few things I need to clear up."

"Come in," I said and showed him to the kitchen. "What's the problem?'

"The problem is I still can't recall how everything happened. The last thing I remember is following you to the marina. Next thing I know, my head is in your lap and you're calling me Jack. I don't like having this loss of memory."

"I've told you. Mrs. North and I spoke to a girl who worked for Hayden. She told us he had a boat at the marina. We thought we'd have a look. Then you showed up. The men came out, you beat them up pretty good. Mrs. North sprayed them in the face with Aqua Net, which is how I accidentally pushed you off the boat. I was trying to protect your eyes."

"You were protecting me, huh? It's my job to be the protector. You should leave chasing bad guys to me."

"It won't happen again," I said and smiled at him.

He smiled back. "Why don't I believe you?"

"Do you want to watch *It's a Wonderful Life* with us?"

"Isn't that a Christmas movie?"

"It's Christmas every day here at North Pole Beach," I said.

We started up the stairs heading for the screening room when we heard a small explosion. The fireworks had begun. I took hold of Detective

Nettles's hand and led him out to the balcony where the others had already gathered.

"Nico paused the movie," Mrs. North told me. "Detective Nettles, how lovely you could join us."

We stood and watched the colors explode over the night sky. Minutes passed before I realized I was still holding the detective's hand.

"Sorry, Detective," I said, and started to pull away, but he held on to my hand.

"I think you can call me Michael."

"Alright, Michael." I looked back at the stars and the fireworks and listened to the sound of the ocean moving against the sand.

I wasn't going to complicate this sweet, simple moment.

The End

Also Featuring This Author

Shell House

Love on the Edge

Over the River and Through the Woods

Into the Woods

The Boardwalk

North by North Pole Beach

About the Author

KIMBERLY KURTH GRAY is a writer of fiction and memoir. She is the recipient of the William F. Deeck-Malice Domestic Grant, a Hruska Fellowship Finalist, and a Wellstone Emerging Writer winner. She lives in Baltimore with her family and her pampered pooch Romeo.

Made in the USA
Middletown, DE
24 July 2023